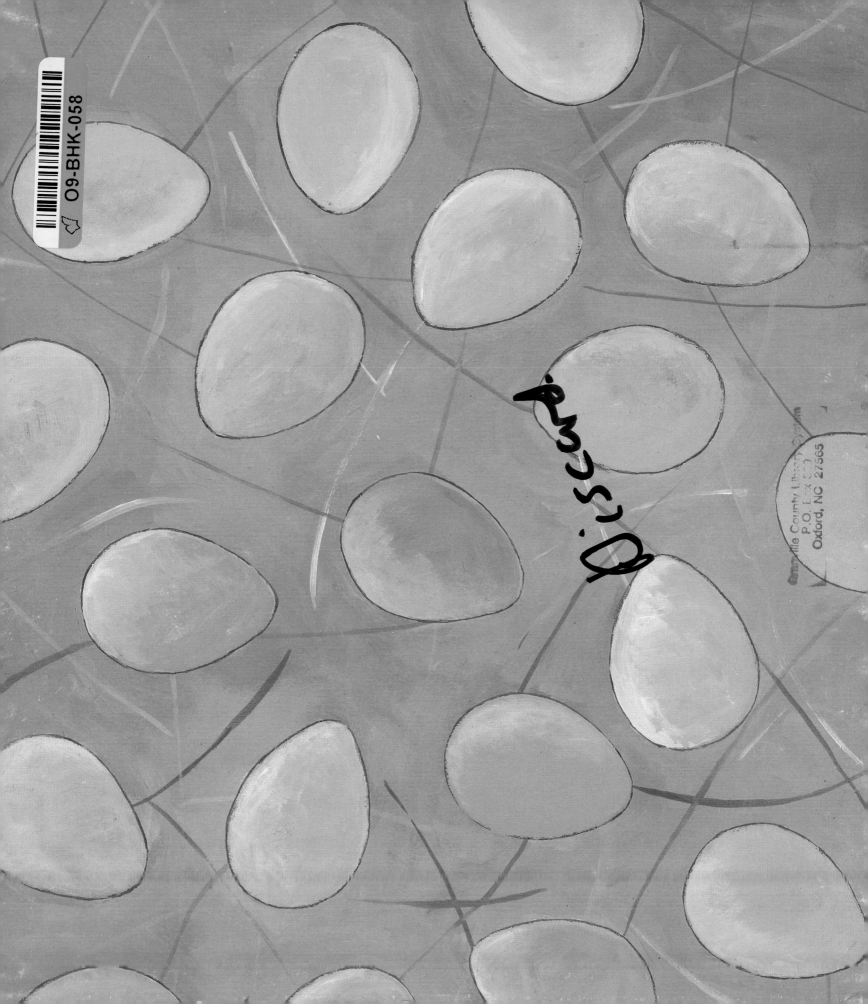

For Timothy
~J.S.

For Emily Anna
~J.C.

First published in the United States 1997 by
Little Tiger Press,
N16 W23390 Stoneridge Drive, Waukesha, WI 53188
Originally published in Great Britain 1997 by
Magi Publications, London
Text © 1997 Julie Sykes
Illustrations © 1997 Jane Chapman

Library of Congress Cataloging-in-Publication Data
Sykes, Julie.
Dora's eggs / by Julie Sykes; illustrated by Jane Chapman.
p.   cm.
Summary : As she goes round seeing the babies of the other
farmyard animals, Dora becomes less and less proud of her
first eggs—until they hatch into cute chicks.
ISBN 1-888444-09-6
[1. Chickens—Fiction.   2. Animals—Infancy—Fiction.]
I. Chapman, Jane, 1970-   ill. II. Title.
PZ7. S98325Do   1997   [E]-dc20   96-34399   CIP   AC

Printed in Belgium
First American Edition
3 5 7 9 10 8 6 4 2

Dora looked at the lambs frolicking in the field. She felt rather glum.

"My eggs are nice," she thought. "But those playful lambs are much nicer."

Very sadly, Dora walked back to the farmyard.

On her way she bumped into Daisy Dog.

"Hello, Daisy," clucked Dora. "Would you like to come and see my eggs?"

"Sorry, Dora," barked Daisy, wagging her tail. "I can't come now. I'm taking my puppies for a walk."

Dora was beginning to feel quite miserable.

"My eggs are nice," she thought.

"But those cute puppies out for a walk are much nicer."

In the farmyard Dora stopped at the cow shed. She wished she felt happier—perhaps Clarissa the Cow would cheer her up.

"Would you like to see my eggs?" she called.

"Shhh," mooed Clarissa softly, nodding at the straw. Snuggled up by her feet was a newborn calf, fast asleep.

Dora wanted to cry.

"My eggs are nice," she whispered. "But that little calf all snuggled up is much nicer."

Dora walked back across the yard in the sunlight and climbed into the henhouse. Her eggs were just as she had left them, smooth and brown and very still.

"My eggs are nice," sighed Dora, fluffing out her feathers. "But everyone else's babies are much nicer."

"Oh no!" cried Dora. "I've broken them!"

Tears began to roll down her face. They splashed onto the nest and over the cracked eggs. As each tear fell, the cracks grew wider and wider until suddenly . . .

. . . up popped a fluffy head,
then another, and another.

Soon the nest was full of tiny chicks.

"Cheep, cheep," the chicks peeped.

"Cheep, cheep."

Dora stopped crying and stared at her babies.

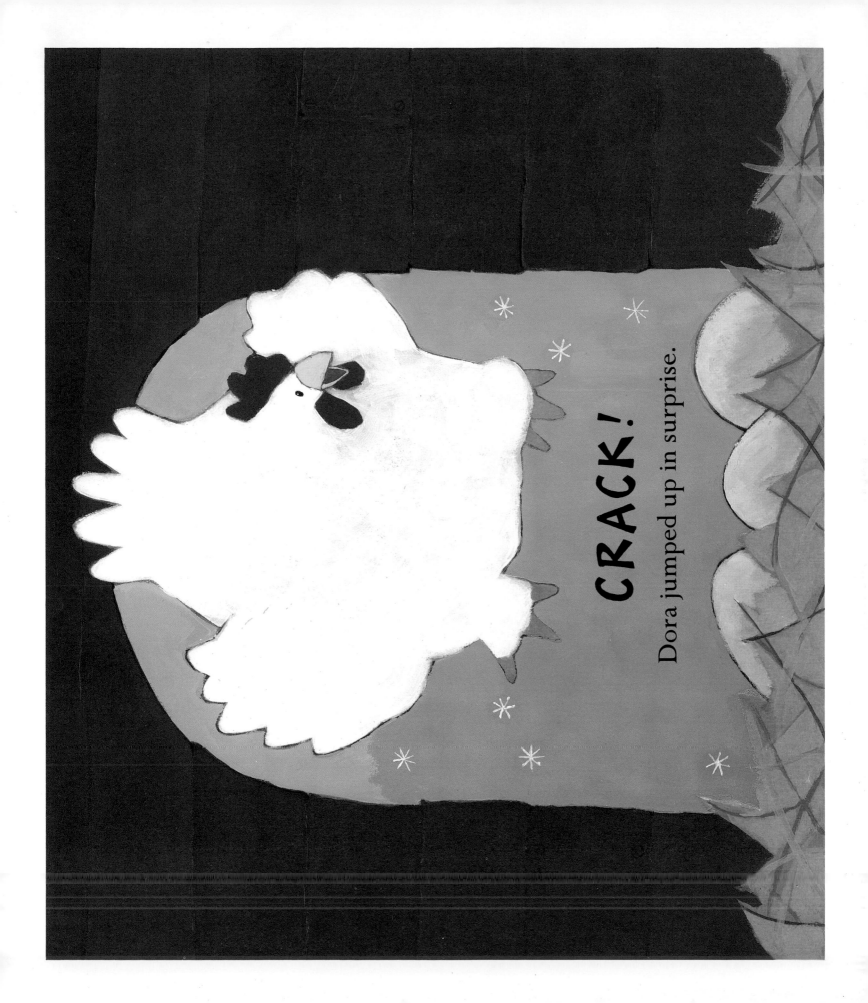

CRACK!

Dora jumped up in surprise.

It didn't matter that the eggs were broken.

The new chicks were everything Dora had ever wanted!

Proudly she strutted out into the farmyard, and one by one the chicks followed after her. All the animals stopped and looked.

"Why, Dora!" quacked Debbie.
"They're as fluffy as my ducklings!"
"And wriggly like my piglets,"
oinked Penny.

"They're as playful as my lambs,"
baaed Sally.

"And you can take them for walks—
just like my puppies," barked Daisy.

"But best of all," mooed Clarissa,
"your chicks can snuggle up to you,
like my calf snuggles up to me."

"Cluck," said Dora happily, agreeing
with her friends. "My eggs were nice,
but my chicks are much, much nicer!"

Very sadly, Dora settled
herself down onto
her nest . . .

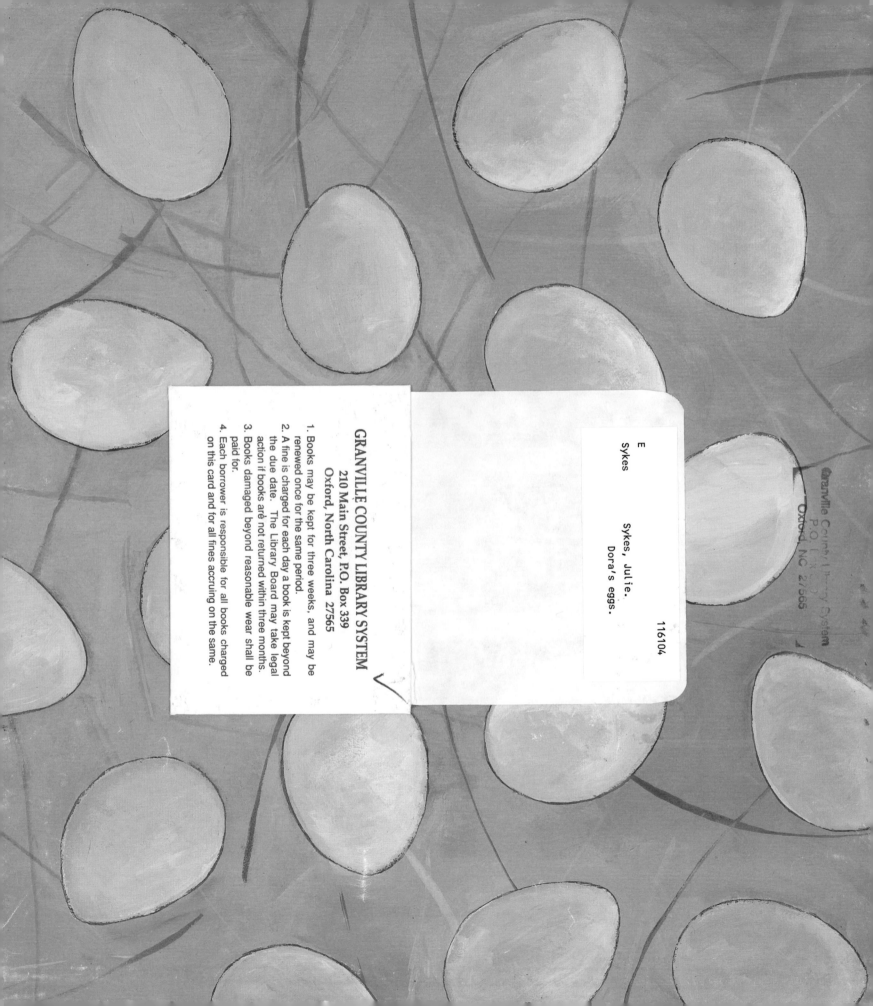

DORA'S EGGS

by Julie Sykes

Pictures by Jane Chapman

Little Tiger Press

Dora was sitting on a nest of eggs.
They were shiny brown and smooth
to touch.

"These are my very first eggs,"
clucked Dora proudly. "I must
get all my friends to come
and admire them."

Dora gave another little sigh as she climbed the hill to find Sally Sheep.

"Would you like to come and see my eggs?" she asked Sally.

"Not today," bleated Sally. "I'm too busy keeping an eye on my lambs."

Dora climbed out of the henhouse and
into the farmyard.
"Who shall I visit first?" she wondered.
"I know! I'll go and find Debbie Duck."

Dora hopped over the fence and across
the field until she reached the pond.

"Hello, Debbie," she called. "Would you
like to come and see my eggs?"

"I can't come now," quacked Debbie.

"I'm teaching my babies to swim."

Dora stood watching the ducklings splashing around and learning to paddle. Somehow she felt a bit less excited. "My eggs are nice," she thought. "But those fluffy ducklings are much nicer."

Dora was just a little sad as she trotted over to the sty to visit Penny Pig.

"Hello, Penny," she clucked. "Would you like to come and see my eggs?"

But Penny didn't hear. She was having too much fun tumbling around with her wriggly piglets.

Dora gave a little sigh.

"My eggs are nice," she thought. "But those wriggly piglets are much nicer."